# PAULA BUNYAN

Phyllis Root

Pictures by Kevin O'Malley

Farrar, Straus and Giroux
New York

To Amelia and Ellen, who heard this story first
—P.R.

To Nora, Margie, Mary Ellen, and Eileen, Paulas one and all!
—K.O.

Text copyright © 2009 by Phyllis Root
Pictures copyright © 2009 by Kevin O'Malley
Distributed in Canada by Douglas & McIntyre Ltd.
Printed and bound in China by South China Printing Co. Ltd.
Designed by Jonathan Bartlett
First edition, 2009
1 3 5 7 9 10 8 6 4 2

www.fsgkidsbooks.com

Library of Congress Cataloging-in-Publication Data
Root, Phyllis.
  Paula Bunyan / Phyllis Root ; pictures by Kevin O'Malley.— 1st ed.
    p.  cm.
  Summary: Recounts the exploits of Paul Bunyan's "little" sister, Paula, who lived in the North
Woods, sang three-part harmony with the wolves, and used an angry bear for a foot warmer.
  ISBN-13: 978-0-374-35759-7
  ISBN-10: 0-374-35759-5
  [1. Tall tales.  2. Size—Fiction.]  I. O'Malley, Kevin, ill.  II. Title.

PZ7.R6784 Pau 2009
[E]—dc22

2007043728

Everyone knows about Paul Bunyan, with his woodcutter's ax and his big blue ox, Babe. But not many people know about Paula Bunyan, his little sister. Maybe "little" isn't the right word. After all, she was as tall as a pine tree and as strong as a dozen moose.

Three times out of six she could outwrestle Paul, and she always outran him. Paula could run so fast that once when she forgot to do her chores, she ran all the way back to yesterday to finish them and got back to today before anyone noticed she was gone.

Being big did have its drawbacks, though. Paula just seemed to have a knack for accidentally busting furniture and knocking over wagons. And when she burst into song, glass would shatter and stone walls crack.

It got so Paula took to humming under her breath instead of singing out loud, just so nobody would holler that she was breaking their windows or chipping their best china.

For a while, Paula had a job running the local ferry. People and cows, barrels and bales, horses and pigs would pile on board. Then Paula would pick up the ferry and carry it across the river. But she got tired of never having any dry socks, and restless from being around so many breakable things.

So after Paul shouldered his ax and
set off to find himself famous, Paula
decided to set off, too. She had a
hankering for the wilderness, for wide,
wild spaces with room enough for her
and her singing.

"We'll pack you a little snack," her ma said, as her parents loaded a sack with two hundred and fifty-three loaves of bread, over a dozen wheels of cheese, several bushels of apples, twenty gallons of cider, and a barrel each of salt and pepper.

Paula set off for the North Woods, where, she had heard, the trees were so tall the clouds got stuck on the tops and a body could go for months without running out of forest to walk through.

She traveled for weeks, till the people thinned out and the trees grew thick. When she came to a place where the water was so blue the fish swam around in the sky and the birds flew around in the lakes because they couldn't tell the difference, she knew she was in the North Woods at last. Paula was so happy she burst into song, starting a moose stampede and knocking eagles out of their nests for miles around.

That first night, she camped by the side of a river. The wolves, smelling something new, came to investigate, nosing around her campfire and howling *Who-roo-roo are you-roo-roo?*

Anyone else might have turned tail and run, but not Paula. She decided those wolves needed a singing lesson or two. By the time the next day dawned, she had them all singing in three-part harmony. After that, the woods rang every night to the singing of Paula and her new friends.

One day, Paula was fishing with her line up in the sky when up walked a black bear, seven feet tall with claws like thirtypenny nails. Anyone else might have crawled up the nearest tree, but not Paula.

When that bear growled, she growled right back.

When that bear smacked a tree trunk, Paula smacked another one. Harder.

They kept it up for a while, growling and roaring and smacking things, when suddenly Paula had a nibble on her fishing line. She excused herself to the bear and pulled in a little northern pike, about a hundred-pounder. The bear roared loud and hungry, but Paula just whopped it on the nose.

"I don't mind sharing if you ask polite-like," she said. "And if you wait till I cook it up with a little salt and pepper."

Pretty soon that bear was following Paula around, leaning up against her while she fished, helping her eat her catch. That bear got so spoiled that whenever they came to a creek, Paula had to carry the bear across just to keep its paws dry.

Lots of folks might have killed that bear and used his skin for a blanket, but not Paula. She used the whole bear for a foot warmer. At night, after a singing session with the wolves, she just pulled him over her feet like a bearskin rug and slept toasty-warm until morning.

Now, folks say the mosquitoes up north are mighty bad, and I believe it's true, because one day a few hungry mosquitoes carried off Paula's bear. Paula wasn't about to see her friend and foot warmer devoured by some bloodthirsty insects. She pulled out the pepper her ma had packed and flung it into the air. You never heard such a sneezing and snorting as those mosquitoes made. They sneezed and snorted that bear loose, and before it hit the ground Paula was there to catch it and fuss over it. That night, their fish didn't taste quite so spicy without any pepper, but neither of them complained.

Paula walked for miles and miles.
Those trees just never seemed to run
out, and neither did her happiness.

But one morning Paula came to the
end of the trees. They didn't just thin
out, they stopped. And where the trees
had stood green and tall, there were
little stumps on the ground. The sight
made Paula sadder than a forest full
of weeping willows.

Paula followed those stumps till she came to some folks who were cutting down trees with their long crosscut saws. As far as the eye could see, the hillside was crawling with fellows with axes and saws, like termites at a timber free-for-all.

Something needed to be done, all right. But what? Paula was big and those fellows were just little bitty mites, but there was only one of her and a lot of them.

Pesky as a bunch of mosquitoes, Paula thought, and didn't that give her an idea.

Back into the woods she went, looking for some of those north-country mosquitoes.

When she finally found a flock roosting by a beaver swamp, Paula stripped down to her skivvies. The sight of all that skin just waiting to be bitten drove those mosquitoes into a frenzy. Paula took off at a slow jog, with those mosquitoes following right after. When she got within a boulder's throw of the lumberjacks, she put on a little burst of speed.

All the lumberjacks felt was a strong breeze as Paula whooshed by. The mosquitoes took one look at those lumberjacks standing there, put on their brakes, and started to feast. Now, these were medium-sized mosquitoes, not much bigger than chickens, but there were enough to drive those lumberjacks wild.

It was too much for the lumberjacks. They took off running like it was payday and never did come back to the North Woods. Paula laughed so hard the birds for miles around took cover, thinking the grandpappy of all storms was blowing their way.

Then Paula got busy replanting trees where those lumberjacks had cut them down and carted them away.

If you're ever up in the North Woods, you might see some of those trees that Paula planted. On a clear night, you might see the light from Paula's campfire flickering against the sky. If you listen carefully, you might hear the wolves howling in three-part harmony.

You might even hear Paula singing, happy in a country just her size.

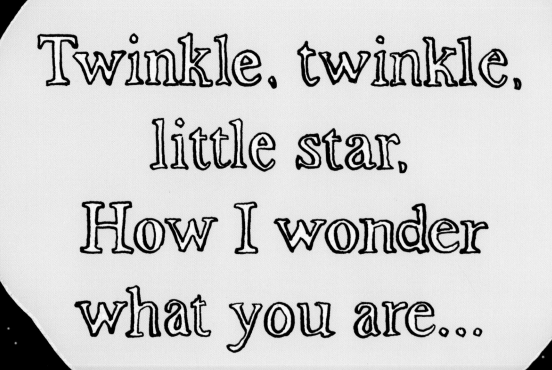